# Snow
# Goalie

WITHDRAWN

WITHDRAWN

# Snow Goalie

## SOPHIE SMILEY

Illustrated by
MICHAEL FOREMAN

Andersen Press
London

First published in Great Britain in 2010
by Andersen Press Limited,
20 Vauxhall Bridge Road, London SW1V 2SA
www.andersenpress.co.uk

British Library Cataloguing in Publication Data available.
ISBN 978 184 939 053 8

Printed and bound in Great Britain by
CPI Bookmarque, Croydon CR0 4TD

*Author's royalties going to The Jean Grove Trust
supporting the education of children in need in Ethiopia.*

*To Christina, Bronwen and Andrew,*
*In memory of David.*

# Chapter 1

"Goal!"

I flew down the pitch, my arms wide like an aeroplane. My brother, Bobby, charged towards me yelling, "Whaddagoal! Here we go, here we go!"

You see, it wasn't just any goal I'd scored; it was the best sort – in the ninetieth minute. The referee's whistle peeped, and we were through to the final.

Mum and Dad invaded the pitch. Then Bobby led the team back to our house singing, "Football's coming home . . ."

That evening we watched the match on video, with lots of shouting: "Good tackle", "What a dive", "Where're your glasses ref?" Everyone erupted when I made my final push down the pitch. We all whooped "Goal!" as the ball bashed the back of the net.

You see, my whole family is football mad. Mum and Dad are so football crazy that they even went to a match on their wedding day. At half-time, Dad asked Mum how many children she wanted, and she said, "Enough for a team!"

And here we are – all with funny football names – and through to the final of the local five-a-side tournament.

My big brother Striker and I play up front (well, with a name like that he couldn't really play anywhere else, could he?); Wembley and Semi are in defence, and Bobby's our goalie. I'm the youngest, then Bobby. We were named after Dad's world cup hero, Bobby Charlton. (Some people think Charlton's a funny name for a girl, but I like being different.)

Well, we'd won the semi final, but we couldn't relax. There was only one week till the final – our biggest match ever. We all had our eyes on the prize, and we were determined to win!

# Chapter 2

The next morning Bobby was up early, kicking a ball into our bunk-bed goal. He didn't want to waste a second's precious practice time.

It had rained all night, so later, when we made our way to the park, we had to dodge puddles. The pitch shimmered. Semi sent a ball skimming across the wet turf, and Bobby ran into goal to stop it. Whoosh! He flew flat out.

"Save," he yelled, as he sank into a ginormous puddle.

"Oh, Bobs," I called, running to help him. Sitting up, he spurted water from his mouth. His lip wobbled. For a moment, I thought he was going to cry. But his face lit up. He dived back into the water, and made windmill movements in the goal-mouth pool.

Then he snapped his arms together and shouted, "Shark attack!"

But soon he was a very shivery shark.

Wembley splashed across the pitch and picked him up. Bobby's teeth were chattering. "Ccold," he stammered.

"Yes, you're freezing," said Wembley, peeling off his wet top.

"Knock knock," Semi distracted him.

"Who's there?"

"Freeze."

"Freeze who?"

"Freeze a jolly good fellow!"

Bobby's chattery teeth chuckled.

Wembley dressed Bobby in a

hoody which came down to his knees. He put a huge pair of gloves on his blue feet, then swung him onto his shoulders. He carried him back to a warm bath singing,

"Freeze a jolly good fellow . . . and so say all of us."

"But what are we going to do?"
I wailed to Dad that evening.
"How can we win the final if we
don't practise? Our pitch is only
good for water polo."

"Don't you worry – it'll be
better by tomorrow," said Dad.

And I believed him. How wrong
could I be?

# Chapter 3

That night, I listened for the rain.
But all I could hear was a strange,
muffled sort of silence. It wasn't
the kind of silence you get before a
penalty shoot out. This was a
silence I'd never heard before.

When morning came, I drew
back the curtain and gasped.

The whole world was white!
Magical.

"Bobby," I called.

He stood beside me, eyes wide as footballs. Normally, Bobby moves about all the time. Even when he's in goal and the play is up the other end, he jigs on the spot. But today he stood ghostly still, staring at the snowy wonderland.

"C'mon," I tugged, and together we charged downstairs, pulling coats and boots over our pyjamas.

Bobby tiptoed across the cold crunchiness. He stopped, turned and studied his footprints. Bending down, he touched the ground warily. Then, grinning, he scooped up a handful of snow and licked it.

"Ice cream," he laughed.

"Knock knock," I said.

"Who's there?"

"Ice cream."

"Ice cream who?"

"Ice cream if you throw me in the snow!"

Bobby shrieked and chased me, yelling "I scream, you scream." He kicked up a snow storm as he ran.

Our neighbour's dog, Davy, squeezed through the fence and ran with us. When we threw snowballs, he jumped up and tried to catch them as if they were sticks.

"Watch this," I said, rolling a handful of snow along the ground.

It grew from a ping pong to a football. Big as a balloon. Bigger still, till it looked like a space hopper. Bobby copied me. A few minutes later, I looked round. The garden was empty. I followed Bobby's footsteps towards the back door. Soggy heaps of snow led up the stairs like Hansel and Gretel's trail of breadcrumbs. A huge scream burst from Mum and Dad's room. I rushed in. Dad's head was covered in snow. He looked like an ice cream cone! Bobby was giggling and singing, "Snowball's coming home, It's comin . . ."

"I'll snowball you!" said Dad, leaping out of bed and chasing Bobby down the stairs. Mum and I watched from the window as Bobby filled a bucket, then dashed up the slide. Dad followed, barefoot. We giggled as he danced dementedly about the garden, shrieking. Davy thought it was a great game, and yelped and bounded after him. Then Dad bent over to make a snowball. Bobby pelted him, Pow – right on the bum!

Mum and I couldn't stop laughing.

Then a horn hooted. Mum gasped, leant out of the window and blew her whistle (she's the referee in our house). "Match over," she called. "Taxi's here."

You see, my brother Bobby has Down's syndrome, and goes to his school by taxi. Sometimes I'm jealous of him getting a ride, but today I was happy to walk to my school, rolling a humungous snowball as I went. It was brilliant. And as I walked, I made plans: I'd build an igloo with Bobby when we got home. I could hardly wait.

# Chapter 4

As soon as school ended, I bolted home. Bobby usually arrives before me, but not tonight. Why was he late? I stomped around the garden, smacking snow into bricks for our igloo, then running out to look for the taxi. The darkness closed in, but it didn't stop me. I found a lantern and carried on building. Perhaps Bobby and I could sleep in our ice house if I worked fast enough.

But something in my tummy started fluttering. A butterfly of worry. Where was my brother? Soon the butterfly had turned into a vulture. I went inside. Mum smiled, but I could tell she was worried too.

Then the telephone rang. Mum picked up the receiver.

She sank into a chair. Something awful had happened.

"Bobby?" I whispered.

"It's all right," said Mum, putting down the phone. "He's fine. Having a great time. It's just that the road is blocked and the taxis can't get through."

"Oh." My face crumpled.

"They've got food and blankets. So they're all cosy and they're going to sleep at school." She tried to sound cheerful, but I could hear the worry wobble in her voice.

"But he's never been away from me," I said, panicking.

You see, Bobby and I do everything together, and no one else understands him like I do.

"He'll be scared. He can't sleep without his mascot. We've got to go and rescue him," I begged.

"He'll be fine," said Dad. "It will be an adventure."

"He'll be home in two peeps of a ref's whistle," said Mum. "Now, cocoa and bed for you."

"But Mum . . ."

"No buts – bed!" she said in her best ref's voice. I knew that any minute now, she'd get out her yellow card. How could she be so cruel?

I couldn't sleep, not without Bobby in the bottom bunk. I just couldn't stop thinking about him. How would he manage without me? I tossed and turned, growing

sadder and sadder as I pictured
him cold, crying and alone. Then,
slowly, a plan grew in my head. It
was a scary plan. Terrifying. But I
had to do it. For Bobby.

# Chapter 5

I had never run away before. But I had no choice. Bobby needed me.

I felt a tingle of fear as I packed my rucksack: Bobby's cuddly dog, Spiderman PJs, and his *Greatest Goalkeepers* book. I put on my warmest clothes and crept downstairs. I could hear Mum, Dad and the big boys cheering. They were watching the football highlights. How could they laugh when Bobby was stranded, cut off from the rest of the team? I choked back tears. Creeping through the kitchen, I picked up Bobby's favourite biscuits and slipped silently out of the back door.

As I set off, I kept expecting Dad to pop up behind me, swing me onto his shoulders and say, "I'm coming with you." But he didn't. Instead, the cold nipped my nose. I tried to sing, "You'll Never Walk Alone", but my croaky voice was snatched away by the wind.

I'd been to Bobby's school for fêtes and fairs, and knew the route.

Well, I thought I did. The first bit was easy, the street lights bright, the white road empty. But as I reached the edge of town, it got harder. My legs grew tired. My feet sank deeper and deeper into the deep snow. Frost crept inside my clothes and pinched me.

Then the road split. Which way was it? It was all so clear in the daytime. A shriek came from the left fork, so without stopping to think, I dived down the right.

It grew darker. There were loads of trees. Black branches hung like skeleton hands. An owl hooted. I jumped. Thoughts of my warm bed, and the family crowded round the telly, flooded over me.

Then, behind me, I heard breathing. Soft at first, then stronger. I walked faster. The rasping sound grew louder. Whoever was following me was getting closer. I tried to run, but it was like one of those nightmares when your legs won't move. Rounding the bend, I froze in my tracks. There, in front, was a man, arms outstretched, waiting.

I was trapped.

# Chapter 6

But I'm a striker. What would I do if this were next week's final and two defenders tried to close me down? My football sense kicked in, and I darted sideways. The giant's arms stretched across my path. I swerved. A final sprint, and I was past him. But the other attacker was still on my heels. Lunging forward, I tripped and sprawled headlong into the snow. The

panting bore down on me. I tried
to scream but my mouth filled
with cotton wool coldness. I put
my hands over my head, and
waited.

Something wet touched my
cheek. Something rough and soft
and sloppy.

There was a gruff bark.

"Davy!"

I rolled over and hugged him, "Oh, Davy Dog," I sobbed into his fur. He wagged his tail and slobbered that he was glad to see me too.

Then I sat up. What about the man, the one who'd blocked my way? Davy pricked his ears up, alert to my fear. He woofed, bounded off and disappeared round the corner.

"Come back," I wailed as his tail vanished.

Sitting in the snow, I felt lonelier than I'd ever felt in my life.

It seemed like hours before Davy returned. He tugged my coat and dragged me back. "No, Davy." I shrank as the bad man came into view.

But Davy bounded forward.

"Come back," I whimpered.

Davy jumped at the man, and bit his nose off. Skipping back, he dropped it at my feet.

I stared down. A carrot. Davy bounded off and pulled a twiggy arm from a snowman!

# Chapter 7

I didn't know whether to laugh or cry. There were no monsters trying to get me, but I was still lost. And Bobby was somewhere in the darkness.

"We must find Bobby," I said to Davy dog. Wagging his tail wildly, he set off.

"Wait for me," I called.

A few minutes later, I heard a wailing sound. It grew louder.

Then there were words: "Snowball's coming home, It's comin' . . ."

"Bobby!" Davy and I tumbled together through the school gates and hammered on the door. A startled teacher let us in. We burst into a classroom where children were settled in sleeping bags, watching *The Snowman*. I looked round the circle. Where was my

brother? A thud, thud sound came from behind me. I turned. There was Bobby, bouncing a ball from knee to knee and muttering, "Nine, ten, 'leven."

When he finally dropped the ball, he looked up and saw us.

"'Ello Charlie, 'ello Davy," he grinned. Then he picked up the ball, held it out to me and said, "Football?"

# Chapter 8

Well, Bobby's teacher blew the whistle on a night game of footie! She phoned home to tell them I was safe, and found me some blankets.

Bobby zoomed about the room being Spiderman, before we snuggled down on the floor. Davy Dog lay in the middle like a hot-water bottle. And then I realised that Dad had been right – it was an adventure.

It was strange to wake up in a classroom. Bright, white light drew us to the windows, and soon we were outside again. On the field, the snow was so deep that Bobby could touch the top of the goal. Together, we built snowmen – a whole row of them across the goal

front. I took free kicks over a wall of carrot-nosed defenders, knocking off five players' heads as I scored my goals!

A shout went up. We turned to see a snow plough scooping its way through the school gates. The driver gave us each a turn in the cab as he cleared the playground; it was brilliant!

Soon the cars arrived, and for the first time in my life, I got to go home in a taxi!

# Chapter 9

It took some time for the snow to melt, so we didn't get back to the park till the day before the final. We desperately needed more training. Even though the snow had gone, it was colder than ever.

We neared the pitch, and it glinted in a glassy kind of way. Bobby ran for goal, but as soon as his boots crossed the touchline, he fell, smack, on his bum. Our football ground had turned from a swimming pool into an ice rink!

But worse was to come. And it came in the shape of Kevin Joggs. His team had got through to the final by cheating. They were top of the league for diving, and dirty tackles.

Cocky Kevin strutted past, calling, "Looosers!" Then his mates started chanting, "You've lost, and you know you have . . ."

A ball of temper bubbled up inside me. I was about to shout back at them when Bobby called over, "Count to ten, Charlie." He always helps me when I'm about to lose it. I remembered Dad's words, "Hold your head high, and walk away."

Kevin's team looked smug. They opened their kit bags, and changed their boots.

"Hey, that's not allowed..."

"You can't play football in skates!"

"Says who?" Kevin glided over to Bobby, and pushed him over. I saw red. All thoughts of counting to ten vanished. Nobody does that to my brother. I charged forward,

fists ready to fly. But as I pulled
back to punch him, the ice zipped
my feet from under me and I fell,
thump, onto my tummy.

Kevin circled skilfully, laughing.

I could beat him in a normal fight, but today I was helpless and he knew it. Semi and Striker teetered across the ice and guided Bobby and me to firmer ground.

We stood, stranded on the touchline, as Kevin's team swooped effortlessly round, passing the ball from skate to skate.

Heads down, we made for home. For once, Bobby wasn't singing and Semi wasn't telling jokes. It was all over. There was no way we could beat them in the final now.

# Chapter 10

I lay on my bed, too fed up even to read a football magazine. Kevin Joggs's smirking face kept invading my head. The thought of him lifting the trophy was horrible.

"Cheer up, Charlie – I've got a plan," said Wembley.

"And me," grinned Bobby.

But nothing could beat those cheats on their skates, I thought, burying my head in a pillow.

In the background, I heard phone calls, and Bobby rummaging in cupboards. But I knew we'd lost.

I went to bed feeling as flat as a punctured football.

Next morning, I woke to the sound of Bobby singing "Frosty the Snowman."

There was Bobby, tying pillows to his tummy with football scarves. Semi found a huge football shirt that fitted over the top, and when Bobby was finally dressed, he was as round as a snowman! But being fatter than Kevin Joggs wasn't going to win us the match, not if we were all flat on our bottoms. It was hopeless.

But, I hadn't reckoned on Wembley. As we set off for the park, he told me his secret. So when I saw Joggs's team gliding across the ice, I felt my first stirring of hope.

"You going to crawl on your bums like babies?" Kevin shouted.

"Oy – look – it's Tweedledum,"
Gary pointed at Bobby.

This time I held my head high.
Smiling, I laced up the strange
boots that Wembley had handed
out. I could hardly wait for Kevin's
face when he saw our secret
weapon.

We made our way onto the icy surface, awkward at first, but moving faster as we grew used to our new feet. I saw a frown cross Kevin's face as we took our positions without falling. The whistle went.

# Chapter 11

Kevin snatched the ball straightaway, swept across the ice and scored. One nil down in the first minute. My hopes melted, and I wished that the ice would too.

But then the opposition started to make mistakes. Kevin whizzed forward and overshot the ball. He looked surprised as I got possession and passed it to Striker. We were getting used to our secret weapon

–spiked running shoes that Wembley had borrowed! As our confidence grew, we surged forward. Paul Parker tackled, but his skate got caught and he flipped onto his back like an upturned woodlouse. Striker shot the ball to the top corner. Their goalie tried to jump, but his arms shot one way and his skates the other. He went splat, and the ball found the back of the net. One all – we were back in the game!

The second half was messy. They glided, but overshot. Kevin couldn't do his usual tripping and diving tricks. But we were slower than them. No one could break free to get a shot on goal.

Then it happened. Kevin saw his chance and grabbed it with both skates. A gap in our defence let him soar forward, bearing down on goal. Bobby jigged awkwardly, uncomfortable in his new boots. Kevin grinned – one on one – his chance to score. Pulling back his foot, he powered the perfect shot.

It soared towards the far post, way out of Bobby's reach. I couldn't bear to watch them win.

But I'd forgotten about Bobby. He launched himself – a flying snowman – right across the goal mouth. He glided over the ice on his pillowy tummy like a human rocket, and knocked the ball into orbit. Our supporters cheered, while Bobby spun round on his big belly singing, "Snowman's coming home!"

It was still one all, as we neared the ninetieth minute.

Striker got the ball. He signalled to me. I moved up, positioning myself carefully. Striker crossed. I did a nutmeg round Paul. I was

through. Then Kevin appeared.
Splat! I was flung across the ice.

"Foul!" cried my brothers in
chorus.

The referee signaled a free kick.
This was our chance!

The opposition made a wall,
and I pictured them as the
snowmen Bobby and I had built at
his school. This row of carrot
noses wasn't going to beat me.

Drawing my foot back, I looped a curving ball, up, up and over their heads. Their goalie slid to the ground, while the ball swung round and swerved sweetly into the net. The ref's whistle went. We'd done it!

# Chapter 12

Wembley and Striker swung me and
Bobby onto their shoulders, and we
held the trophy between us as we
made for home. Mum had prepared
a special celebration tea. There was
a plate of snowball meringues,
bowls of popcorn snowflakes and
a white cake decorated as a football
pitch. She'd even made a bowl of
jelly into an ice rink, with little
figures skating across it.

We all sat down, hungry, and ready to tuck in. All except Bobby. Where had he got to?

A humming came from the kitchen. I followed the sound. The freezer door stood open, and there was Bobby, sitting on the floor with a tub of ice cream. He stood

up, smiled, and held our trophy aloft. Inside, was a huge ice cream snowman! He carried it proudly to the table and we all joined in as he sang, "Oh when the saints, Go sliding in, Oh when the saints go sliding in!"

## About the Author

*Sophie Smiley was born in a Dominican monastery – she says she had a very happy childhood surrounded by Fra Angelicos and Ethiopian priests! She now teaches English and is also a staff member of Forest School Camps, working with both the able and those with learning difficulties. She is married and has two children and they all live in Cambridge.*

## About the Illustrator

*Michael Foreman is one of the most talented and popular creators of children's books today. He has won the Kate Greenaway Medal for illustration twice and his highly acclaimed books are published all over the world. He is married, has three sons and divides his time between St Ives in Cornwall and London.*

# Have you read the other books about Bobby, Charlton, and their football-mad family?

ISBN 9781842701782  £4.99

## Bobby, Charlton and the Mountain

Bobby wants a football kit for the Queen's visit to his school! Money-making muddles, a beastly bully, and a breathtaking penalty shoot-out lead to a VERY unexpected meeting . . . !

ISBN 9781842704202  £4.99

## Man of the Match

Bobby and Charlie are off to summer camp. As soon as Bobby sees Paul, he insists on being best friends with him, even though Paul hides under his parka. Of course Bobby insists on playing football with Paul whatever the planned activity really is. Charlie has her work cut out to keep track of them – and she has a big challenge of her own, too – a relay race over water, and she's petrified!

### Team Trouble

Bobby and Charlie are terribly concerned when big-brother Semi gets ill. He becomes incredibly grumpy, and will only grunt at people – and worst of all, he doesn't seem to like football any more. Whatever can be wrong with him? Will the girl he meets mysteriously help bring him back into the family team?

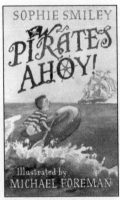

ISBN 9781842706848  £4.99

### Pirates Ahoy!

Charlie's football-mad family have moved their pitch to the beach, and her brother's on a quest for a pirate adventure. It's all hands on deck as footballs become cannonballs and damsels in distress are rescued. But will Bobby ever find his hidden treasure? And will Charlie ever win him back to football?

ISBN 9781842708828  £4.99

### Pup on the Pitch

Bobby's football team has a dog mascot, and he dreams of a cuddly puppy who will join him as a defender on the pitch. But when a real dog arrives next door, he finds it terrifying. Can he overcome his fear? Will he be able to help his sister Charlie in her cup final?

ISBN 9781842708835  £4.99